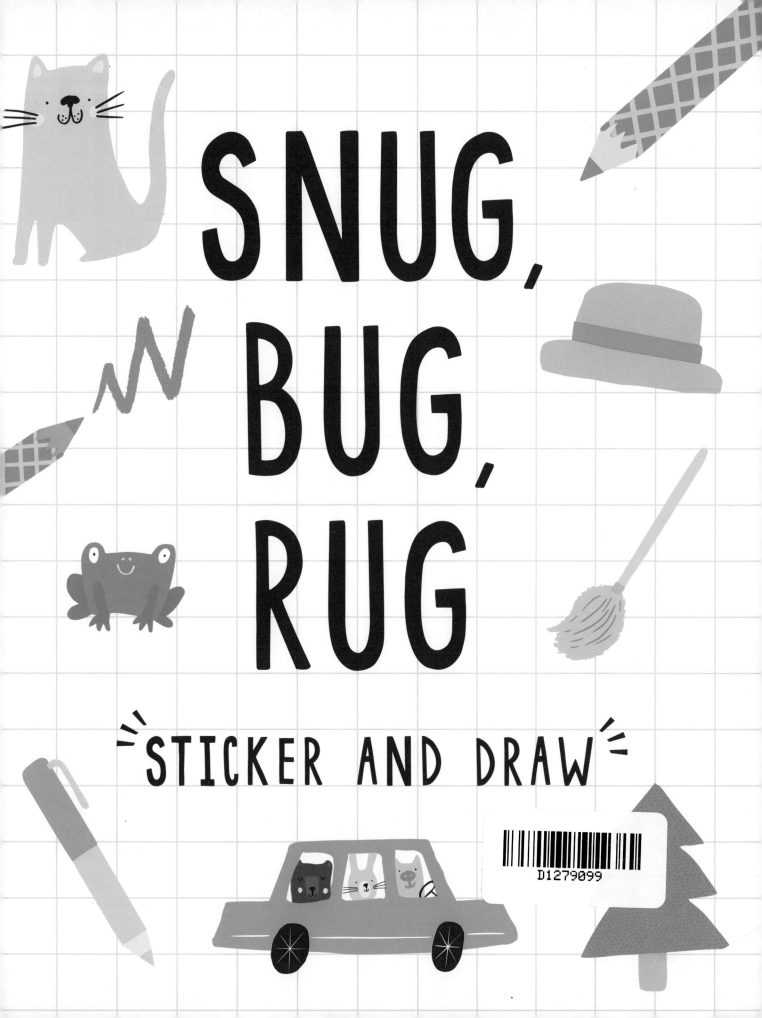

SNUG, BUG, RUG

STICKER AND DRAW

tree

car

map

cat

sock

frog

This edition published by Parragon Books Ltd in 2016 and distributed by

Parragon Inc.
440 Park Avenue South, 13th Floor
New York, NY 10016
www.parragon.com

Copyright © Parragon Books Ltd 2016

Written by Susan Fairbrother
Illustrated by Abigail Burch and Ana Seixas
Edited by Laura Baker
Designed by Karissa Santos and Clare Phillips
Consultant checked by Geraldine Taylor
Production by Charlotte McKillop

ISBN 978-1-4748-2052-3

Printed in China

house

SNUG,
BUG,
RUG

sun

cloud

Note:
To get the best learning
out of this book, it is
recommended
that an adult work
alongside the child.

mop

PaRragon

Bath · New York · Cologne · Melbourne · Delhi
Hong Kong · Shenzhen · Singapore

pen

Look, a cloud that looks like a **cat**!
Sticker other objects you can see in the clouds.

cat

flower

umbrella

tree

hat

key

Whose home is whose?
Sticker the pets!

Curly,
wurly
fur!

dog

dog house

cushion

cat

fish

bowl

hutch

Dotted spots!

rabbit

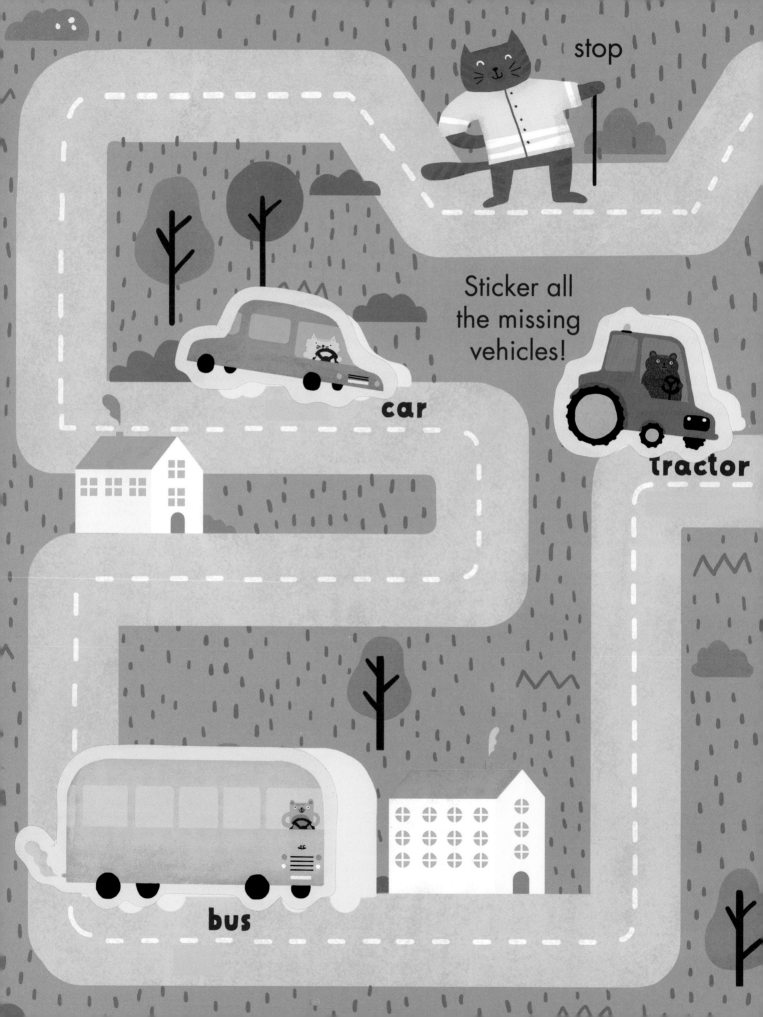

stop

Sticker all
the missing
vehicles!

car

tractor

bus

A sailor went to sea, sea, sea,
To see what she could see, see, see ...

bird

sail

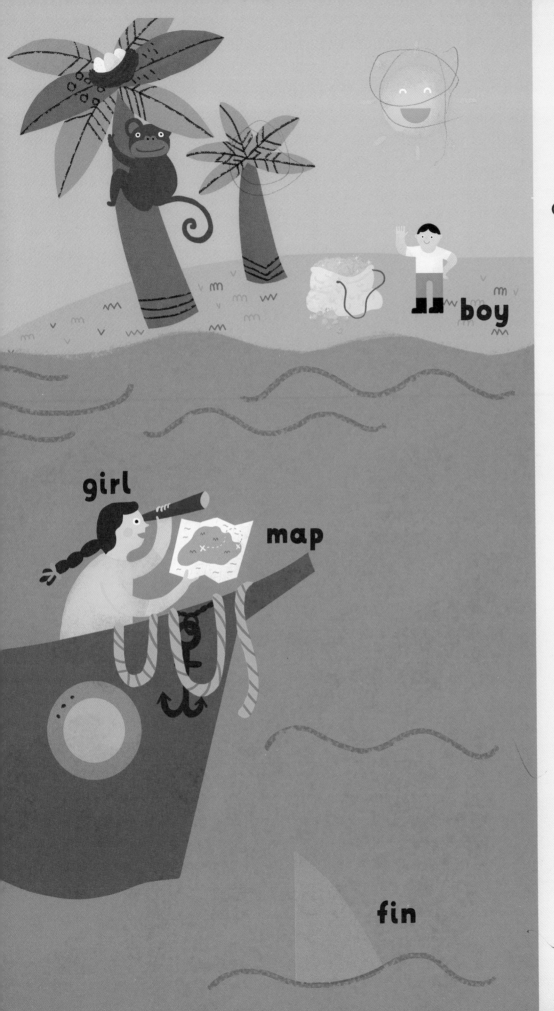

boy

girl

map

fin

What can you see, see, see? Circle these objects in the picture, then check them here:

☑ bell

☑ sun

☐ tree

☐ cat

☐ fish

Hide-and-seek!

Find and trace the letters
in the picture.
Then write them here to
complete these words.

_ **o g**

_ **a t**

_ **e n**

_ **o p**

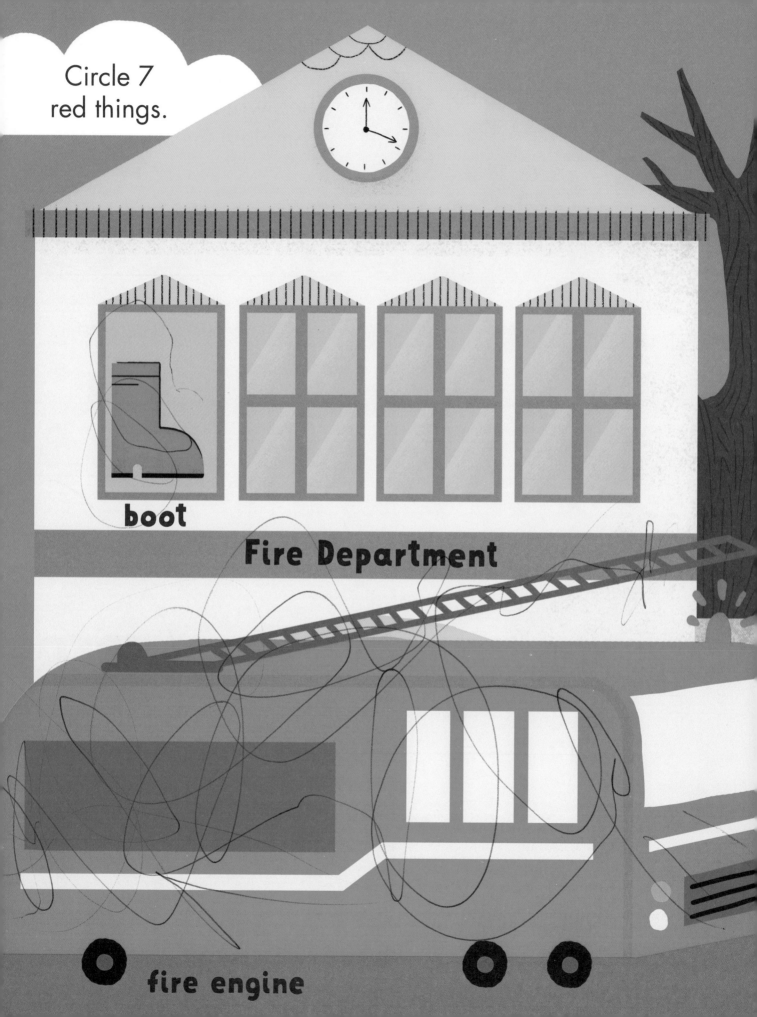

Circle 7
red things.

boot

Fire Department

fire engine

balloon

mug

hood

stop

hose

Sticker the missing animals.

bug on a rug

dog on a log

bird in
a nest

fox in a
box

frog
on a
log!

What's the weather today?
Draw and stick.

rain
Make it wet.

Doodle and color.

wind
Make it blow.

Stick.

sun
Make it hot.

Trace.

snow
Make it snow.

Pigs **LOVE** mud.
Stick on some splats.

pig

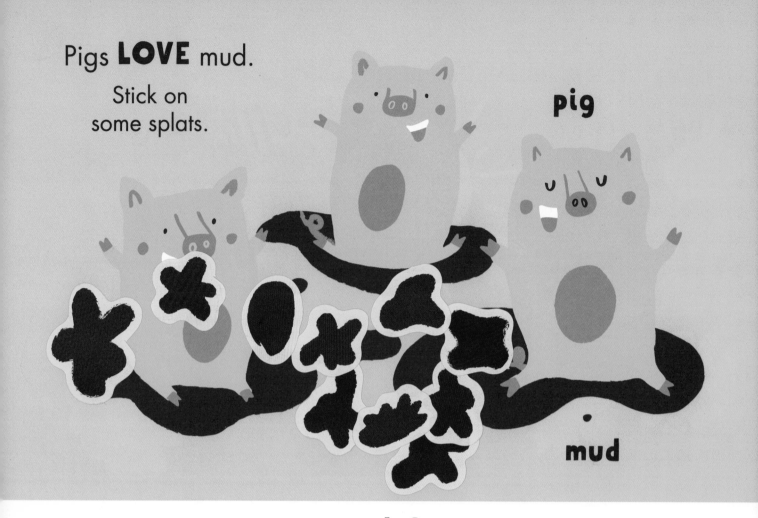

mud

Now clean them up in the **tub** with bubble stickers!

10 hens!
Count them and
sticker the scenes.

1 hen on a **hill**

1 hen in
a **car**

3 hens on a **bus**

2 hens under an **umbrella**

1 hen in a **boat**

ZZZZZZZzzzz

1 hen
in her
bed

1 hen in a **den**

Ten hens in all!

Who is at the door?

It's the …

big bad
wolf!

Follow the path that leads the three little pigs to their safe brick house.

log house tree

5, 4, 3, 2, 1, go!

star

Sticker the stars in the sky and a rocket zooming through space.

Zoom!

rocket

Color the
planets.

Who's on the **mat**?

cat

hat

Where is the rat's **hat**?

rat

Who's on the **plane**?

cat · bat · mouse

Who's **snug** on the **rug**?

bug

These sharks love to make words!

Trace the letters and trails they have made.

Opposites camp!

Big and little

big

little

Find and check the opposites!

big car

little car

big tent

little tent

big fire

little fire

big pan

little pan

big teakettle

little teakettle

big flower

little flower

big butterfly

little butterfly

Welcome to the shop of many things!

pots and pans

bags

mats

fans

Stick more items in each room.

zippers

pets

wigs

(mugs)

Fairy Tale Forest

Help the princess find her way to her castle. Sticker what she sees along the way!

wizard

cave

wolf

giant

troll

witch

fairy

Cute kittens!

They are ...

fluffy

warm

~~slimy~~

cuddly

scaly

cold

soft

pink

Feed the monster with stickers,
and check off as you go ...

cheese and **peas**

socks, **clocks**, and **rocks**

a **bat** and a **hat**

a **shell** and a **bell**

a **mug**, a **pitcher**, and a **rug**!

happy

Stick the faces in the right places.

sad

funny

cross

Presents!

Thank you for my ...

bell

Thank you for my ...

carrot

Thank you for my ...

pen

Thank you
for my ...

hat

Thank you
for my ...

teddy bear

Thank you
for my ...

bun

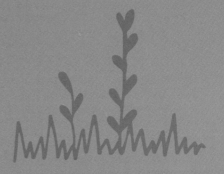

Does the cat look ...

happy

or

sad?

Circle the right word.

He's sad!
He wants a
makeover.

How about
a **hat**?

A **cap**?   A **crown**?

No? How about a big **grin**!

Draw it on.
That's better!

king

Who is wearing
these crowns?

queen

flag

Sticker the very grand,
very shapely home of the
king and **queen**.

window

door

flower

path

dog

tree

frog

hat

cat

car

hen

moon

sock

shell

bell